Storylandia

The Wapshott Journal of Fiction

Issue 9

The Wapshott Press

Storylandia, Issue 9, The Wapshott Journal of Fiction, ISSN 1947-5349, ISBN 978-0-9848325-7-6, is published at intervals by the Wapshott Press, PO Box 31513, Los Angeles, California, 90031-0513, telephone 323-201-7147. All correspondence can be sent The Wapshott Press, PO Box 31513, LA CA 90031-0513. Visit our website at www.WapshottPress.com This work is copyright © 2013 by Storylandia. The Wapshott Journal of Fiction, Los Angeles, California. "Rose" is copyright © 2013 Rebecca Lartigue and is reprinted here with the copyright owner's permission. Copyright for the cover artwork is held by the artist and is reprinted here with the copyright owner's permission.

Storylandia is always seeking quality original short stories, novelettes, and novellas. Please have a look at our submission guidelines at www.Storylandia.WapshottPress.com or email the editor at editor@wapshottpress.com

Many thanks to William Akin for the proofread and editorial support.

Cover: "Rose" by Jennifer Bentson, www.JenniferBentson.com

Storylandia

The Wapshott Journal of Fiction

Founded in 2009

Issue 9, Spring 2013

Edited by Ginger Mayerson

Table of Contents

Rebecca Lartigue

Rose

He doesn't seem as arrogant as the other princes I've known—unsure of himself too, the way he fumbles with his coin. This is not routine to him.

I do not leave my window. Already I think of it as "my" window, though I have just moved into the room this morning, finally convincing Madame that I have earned the privilege. It's not really a privilege: the real reason she has given in to me on this matter is that by standing here, I will be the candle that attracts the moths.

This particular moth is evaluating his first impressions of me. An hour before, he stood there in the courtyard below, I just a silhouette above him instead of this warm, perfumed flesh near him.

Still, he has not yet crossed the room. Most men cannot wait to put their hands on me, to begin to take their money's worth. This one just stands there.

My pride—it stings. I hate him a little already.

Instead of showing this though, I let my voice stroke him from a distance. "You are handsome," I say, for I know that princes, like other men, prefer to think themselves irresistible.

"There's no need for flattery," he says, curt.

I realize then how much a boy he still is. Or, to be clearer: though he may be nearly my age, I am older than him than can be counted by minutes alone. I have been at Madame's for three years, and he has just seen his first fighting. Hours ago on the field, he grappled with his weakness, probably for the first time.

After feeling such helplessness, most men want to remind themselves of their power. I know better than to mock at such a moment. But I mock, anyway. "You're young, too."

His scabbard clinks against mail, and without looking, I know his hand is on his hilt. I smile that I have vexed him.

He says, "I have killed," as if this fact should make me respect him, or at least fear him. As if in this world *that* were anything to boast of.

The sun is wilting below the horizon and I take a final look out the window for which I have so long campaigned. The view was baptized in blood today. Carrion birds swoop in the day's last light, and the ditch diggers are laying the dead to rest. His people won the battle, but it looks like no one's victory.

There is a leaden feeling in my belly. The fallen are nameless to me and I do not mourn them, exactly. Rather I am remembering the time I crossed that field, in the time before his kingdom's war came here: about the time of *my* kill, and my flight, and how I lost what I carried, leaving nothing to bury. A nothing that felt so very heavy.

I turn back to the room, matching my eyes against the prince's. His are gray.

I need him to know I am not afraid. "Many of us have killed," I say and gesture where he should place his coin.

He sets it down and I walk to the door and slide the bolt. Next to him now, I take his hand and study his signet ring: a boar, his family crest. He has washed most of the dirt and blood from his hands, but a line of grime remains under his nails. He is tall and his breath is warm on my neck.

I have let my robe fall open a little. But when I tilt my face up to his, it is my fine bed he is looking at, not me.

Another sting to my pride. "How many nights since you slept in a bed?"

"Many."

"Poor prince," I say.

Provoked by my tone, he reaches for me finally, but he is still armed and dressed. A movement of my hand arrests him. I gesture to the bench, direct him. "Lay your things there."

I could have helped him—I have taken the armor from many men over these years—but it pleases me to watch. I am feeling my power and his helplessness. This war, at least, has brought new accents, new bodies, to the city.

He wrestles the mail over his head and it clatters the way that it does; then he unlaces the padding and shrugs out of it, and pulls the tunic over his head.

I let my eyes run freely over him. He is trim and his skin is like a child's, barely scarred. I smile a little, certain his nurse must be the last woman to see him naked.

There have been enough preambles. I close the space between us and whisper. "Today you have killed. But have you ever loved?"

His eyes glance down the length of me before retreating to my face. He is almost blushing—a boy, indeed. This virgin-prince amuses me, and it has been a long time since I was amused. But for this blush, I begin to pity him. I think that I should go easier with him, show him the way. I speak before he has to answer my last taunt. "Let us see how *gentle* you can be." I start to kiss his mouth and run my hand over his stomach.

At first he is so reluctant, so cool, it is like kissing a ghost, but then his body begins to respond. I sit on the bed and coax him next to me, and he relaxes a little more, reaching. But still, he is deliberate. As careful as a man walking across a slippery stream.

I was sure I knew his story—certain that he hesitated for the betrayal he was about to wreak on some girl, miles away, who would never know of his break of faith. With the young foreigners who come through Smithton, there is always some girl, miles away. The old ones have learned to manage their guilt.

I couldn't resist tormenting him one last time before I would drive all thoughts of this girl from his head. "And where is she now—the one you are thinking of?" My whisper buzzes in his ear like a mosquito and my hands move over his body.

"Dead," he says.

Men blurt many things in my bed. Few are to be believed, but this is truth.

I lost my course a little, then.

He covered my mouth with his own, to stop any more cruelty from coming out of it, perhaps, but the desperation with which he took me to him sufficed to end all my teasing.

When he first entered my room, I had not understood how much sadness he wore. But when he lay over me, the weight of what he carried—then I recognized it. Only grief and the betrayal of hope feel so heavy.

And there was something in how he clung to me, like a doomed man clings to the wreckage of a ship—out of instinct, more than hope for the shore. Resigned, like he no longer believed there was any shore to make toward.

He *was* gentle enough in the end. But when we were done, he fell asleep holding me like that: so tightly my skin first blanched, then bruised.

By morning his hold has relaxed, the way an old knot loosens over time.

He sleeps on his side, one hand on my thigh, his face before mine. He does not snore. His forehead is smooth. His face is just a sketch, not yet a map.

When he wakes, I see it all in his eyes: the traces of dream still upon him, the girl he was imagining he was with, another where and when. He has been far away—in the past with her, or in some future that would never now exist.

Delusion sheets away from him like water when you rise from a bath, and disappointment settles in its place. He dresses and leaves without saying another word.

Millie brings up my drink and breakfast, and I rise so she can collect the bedding.

I sip the potion, guarantee against complications. The bitterness used to bother me, but I am used to it now. I hand her the empty cup, and she starts downstairs for the laundry.

I go to my window and push back the shutter. Beyond the city wall there is the awkward flap of birds' wings near the ground. Last night's graves have been filled in, but the field is so muddy that it's difficult to see where the earth was turned over itself. How long before anything grows there again? Less time than will seem fitting. The ground does not remember what passed over it.

I pull my robe around me and go downstairs.

I like these morning moments when the House is quietest. The men leave and the other girls sleep. The maids are sweeping out the hearths and mopping the tiles; in the laundry, a girl is moving a paddle around the great vat. They work silently, careful not to lose our good graces, and thus tips and favors. Soon deliveries will start arriving from the vintner, bakers, and butchers, and deliverymen will linger to steal peeks of the women they can't afford.

Madame is in her office already. Like me, she's an early riser, despite being the last to leave the hall each night. Her blue eyes like a physician's inspect us girls for signs of illness or dotage, like that cow-eyed look Iris started to wear my first summer here, after the governor's son singled her out—that summer before he married, *not* Iris, of course, but rather a noble girl with both title and honor intact.

I give Madame nothing to worry about.

"Well?"

"First-timer," I say.

She nods, adds my coin to her coffer, and enters a number in her ledger. I am more than earning my keep, worth her investment—one of the reasons she gave me my nicer room and its window. She has several more years of profit out of me, if I manage to avoid the pox.

I am generally satisfied, as well. Noble manors—the few Qwelli ones I've seen, at least—are no grander than Madame's House, and she is fair to us. We do not work for more than one guest each night, nor do we work every night, these civilities being part of what distinguishes Houses from common brothels, and what distinguishes Pretty Ladies (for so we are called) from whores. We have abundant food and wine, servants and comfortable beds, as well as clothes a duchess would envy.

She is called May, and though she's no longer as young or fresh as her name, she's still as full of license. May is not her given name, of course. No Pretty Lady uses her given name. I am called Rose; that name goes to the girl considered first in a House. I've been Rose for twenty-six months, since the previous Rose moved on to a larger House in Ez.

The use of a false name helped me in the beginning. I was called Violet then. Madame's wine, stronger than anything I'd ever sipped back at the village, helped, too. Thus I barely remember those first hours dining and dancing with clients in the Great Hall, nor those hours afterwards, upstairs in the room.

The waking, though—that I remember. Walls frescoed with scenes that just a day before had made me blush. Incense like the whole world was full of flowers. Bed linens, soft and smooth as the down on a chick... and a hot, hairy, pink body pinning me to the mattress.

But it was as if I wasn't there, not really. I woke with those words galloping through my head: *This is not me. I am not here. This is not me. I am not here.* That incantation held me together sufficiently until the man rose, dressed, left his tip, and said good-bye.

The next night, when the next man closed the door, I was not as drunk as I had been the night before. But I called up those words again, and the spell worked; my body was there, doing and having done, but *I* was elsewhere, hidden away like a love note in a bird nest.

Each morning of that first week I woke beside a snoring merchant or bureaucrat who was neither too old nor too ugly. Madame arranges it so, to ease new girls to the work. I was quite awkward: raw as some of those I've seen come to work for Madame since. A few of the girls, ruined or ruining themselves before their families could arrange marriages, come from the same high social classes as our clientele. *They* come with the right accents. The rest of us Madame must transform, dusting off the country, dressing us like our betters, and seeing that we learn a bit of poetry and music, as well as how to dance and play cards.

She teaches us many things: when to speak and when to be silent, what men want and what pleases them. For as alike as most men are, they want slightly different things: merriment or earnestness, attention or scorn. They are attracted by faces or bosoms or legs. They might be drawn in by forwardness or modesty, by wit or wine, by refined music or bawdy jokes.

Madame and her lessons showed me the way in my new life at the House, but I would have had a much harder time adjusting were it not for one of the girls. Luna was her name—her name here, at least. She was a village girl, like me, and she became a friend. It was she, actually, and not Madame who gave me the best advice about handling the men. At first I was polite with them—shy, even. But Luna said to be mean and tease, else they would forget the way things were supposed to be at a House. And she was right; my dealings went far easier after I started acting as she advised.

She was smart, and sharp-tongued, and so merry. On our way down to the hall each night, we used to trade whispers about the men waiting, who we glimpsed through the banisters—just enough observations to make the other one giggle. How lightly she took it all! She used to laugh about her small little self making such great men beg!

I miss her.

It is afternoon, and the House is not yet open. In the hall, Pearl and Ivy play cards; Lily practices her lute. I take a book from Madame's library to my room and try to read. But I am on the same page hours later when the sun starts to disappear.

The winter day has drained away, and like most days, I can't account for it. From my window I watch carts leave the city for the night. I have seen so little of the world. I try to imagine what brings all these people to Smithton and what carries them off. I wonder about the cozy homes they are going to, and what it would be like to be the lady of one of those houses.

Within the city walls, townsfolk leave off their business and return home. A striped cat waits on the doorstep of the widow's house across the way, and the dark-haired daughter of the jeweler next door returns from her lessons and kisses her father and mother. On the street, peddlers pack up their carts and wares, and noblemen and noblewomen ride by, haughty in their furs.

The women do not pause; they ride coolly past our gate. Yet the boldest do steal glances at the House, for they are curious about us Ladies. Are we happier than they? Do we see more of their men than they do? They wonder if we are the daughters cast out of the family house, the sisters and cousins who went away quietly and never returned?

The men pause and look up to this window above the entryway, where I stand. A sheer curtain is all that is between me and Madame's inviting courtyard. My hair is down and I wear a tight-laced dress that shows off my figure because light from the room silhouettes me. The House will open soon.

Come, moths.

A week after the Wahnese victory, our regular clientele of Qwelli officers and city leaders are still absent, licking their wounds. Some locals resent the region falling to Wahnese control, but they have no choice but to accept matters. The battle was lost, the city taken. I hear there are uprisings in a few neighborhoods, but these are quickly put down.

For their part, the Wahnese are remarkably orderly. Professional, like they have done this many times before, wrecking no more than they have to.

The hall is full of them tonight. Some sit at tables with Ladies, eating, drinking, and playing cards. Others dance, holding tight to the girl they will have. A number of Wahnese officers eye me, but I am waiting for Madame to assign me.

I don't mind the Wahnese. As clients, the conquerors have the liveliness and generosity of those far from home who have recently seen death. They are generally easy to satisfy.

Indeed, most of the men who visit us are tolerable, no worse than dull. Coming to a House, and paying what they pay—not just to take us to bed, but also to eat and drink, converse and gamble—they are looking for something more refined than the whore they could have for a quarter hour and fraction of the price down at the neighborhood tavern, or in a back alleyway. No, these men want an experience: music and dancing, a bath and a clean bed. They want to boast and tell their stories, then coax silks off soft, willing limbs. They want to be pleasured by a pretty face, tickled with clean hair.

True, some are sour-breathed. Corpulent. Sweaty. Hairy. The worst kind of client is the newly-rich, or those who have married into status. Madame says their money is as good as the others', and she always likes to cultivate new customers. But we girls know the trouble these men are. They feel compelled to demonstrate how below them you are, even if you were once village neighbors. Their insecurity comes across in every interaction—the fear they are being tricked when you play cards, and that the steward is pouring them the lesser vintage. And then there is their greed for pleasure: they always suspect you are withholding from them some unknown, greater delight, on purpose.

No, we prefer the nobles, officers, and merchants; these understand how Houses work. And the merchants are by far the easiest. They are used to buying and selling, and they tend to be clearest about terms.

The music is loud, but different strands of laughter weave over it; and whenever a Lady crosses the Hall, she leaves a trail of perfume. Finally the man Madame has been expecting arrives—an ambassador from Maritea. She signals me, and I go to welcome him. He kisses my hand reverently. I brush snow from his hair, snake my arm around his, and take him to a table beside the fire.

A few cups of wine later, he is at ease. He leans to me and whispers, "Mistress Rose, I bleed for you. I loved you the moment I lay eyes on you."

"So long?" I always smile as if I have not heard these lines before. I let him touch my thigh beneath the table and ask what brings him to Smithton. He tells me his story, as they always do.

The night grows old. Coral and Iris have already gone upstairs, but Ivy is with a foreign lieutenant who has lost too much gambling to walk with her to a room. Before she goes off with someone else, her smiling red mouth rests at his ear: she is letting him understand exactly what his losing has cost him tonight, but if he returns tomorrow...

That smile, such a snare.

The room has thinned out, and I notice the Wahnese prince I entertained last week. I did not see him come in, and I point a welcoming smile in his direction. If he asks for me, Madame will give another girl to the ambassador. But when the prince sees me, he looks away and quickly chooses someone else. Ivy, I think.

I could be insulted, but I just laugh like Luna taught me.

Later that night, I am dreaming, and the one I love—loved—is there.

I dream it is almost summer, about to rain, and he and I are alone under the pear tree where we used to leave notes for one another. The wind is whipping, but we don't care that the rain is going to catch us because it is so warm and we are so young. His hands snag in the tangles in my hair and his lips are on my neck. I feel dizzy, like I'm on the edge of cliff, but he is holding me up against him, I will not fall. The wind throws down white petals and a soft rain sticks them to my breasts, bare for his kisses—and his hair, black as a crow's wing, even shinier in the rain, is so smooth under my hand. He is pressing against me—and, oh!— the fevered sweetness of it!

I wake flushed, my heart racing; there is a sour taste in my mouth. The darkness is still full and there is no moon, and no rain, and no pear tree, and I remember that I am with the ambassador from Maritea. He is passed out on his side of the mattress, unaware of me.

Noiselessly I climb out of bed, steal to the window, and push back the shutter. I want the air, sharp and calming.

I have not dreamed this dream for a long time. In truth, it is more a memory than a dream. I like to believe that I have trained myself not to think any more of this boy or of the future I'd imagined for us. But somehow the memory has resurrected itself, like a stubborn weed.

Before I can stop myself, I am wishing for a cool hand to lay across my forehead and over my eyes— wishing that someone would say my name, softly, in the dark. There is no point to wishing, though. This is no fairy tale.

The bed frame creaks. The ambassador has turned with a snort and looked up from his pillows. His voice is groggy but his tone is firm: "Back to bed, girl."

I close the shutter and return.

After the Maritean departs, leaving an additional shining coin on the table, Millie comes up with my morning potion. It is lukewarm— again—and I snap at her. I drink it off in two gulps, hand her the cup, and tell her to come back later for the sheets.

Her fingers wiggle as she leaves, tallying the days of the month. It is not that, though I can offer no reason for my peevishness.

I pull the blanket around me, taking it all for myself, and curl into a ball. I should have asked Millie to feed the fire before she left. I know I would be warmer if I got up to put on another log, but I lack the will to move.

I am thinking about the morose prince who was with Ivy last night and me last week, his eyes as gray and gloomy as the coin the ambassador left. The prince left no morning gift (so much a first-timer!) but he certainly was generous in spreading his sadness about: it is as if he left open some door that has allowed unfutured dreams to sneak in here. I think that is what chills me, and the room, more than the cold outside.

Exhausted, I close my eyes, and I wake to voices—the girls, gathering below in the hall for the evening's guests.

A voice calls from the passageway, moving toward my room: "Rose? Where is Rose?"

It's one of the servants. The sunlight has moved to the other side of the room, where it is dying. I have slept the whole day and it is nearly time to receive another man in my bed.

"Tell Madame she is coming," I say.

I was dreaming of carrion birds and rose-tinted bath water, and the vegetable garden at my mother's house. I gulp a glass of wine, straighten my dress, comb my hair, and start down, but I am unlucky enough to pass Madame herself on the landing.

"You're late."

Madame hates tardiness. "I'm sorry."

"Perhaps your new room is too far from the hall? You cannot hear when you are called?"

I lower my eyes. "No, Madame. It won't happen again."

She pulls her lips tight, like the string around a coin purse, and nods. "You will entertain the General tonight."

The General is a feeble old Qwelli with foul breath and an ulcerous leg. Naturally he visits the House religiously. As he has no preference, Madame makes the girls take him in turns. I haven't had to entertain him for almost two years, not since I took my title. Madame's order is my punishment for being late.

I keep my eyes down, humble. "Yes, Madame."

To my surprise, her hand touches my face and

the shadows of my confused dreams start to leave my head. Her touch says I will soon be forgiven, and my smile is almost real with relief.

Madame is usually all business, and there is iron in her, but she can be kind, too. Like last spring, when I was ill for a week—she nursed me herself. I was so delirious I could not even remember what my mother used to call me.

As I walk down to the hall, pushing memories back into distant corners, I am thinking that I need to find that forgetting again. Forgetting is what is necessary.

I join the others, playing cards with clients and acting merry, killing time until the General arrives. Then he sits beside me and I turn my smiles to him. The server brings us our plates. As we eat, he is telling me every detail of his consultation with a physician in Qwel. I listen; my patience has been paid for. I am agreeing that his color does indeed look better since the last time he visited us, when a young man enters the hall, raucous with his friends, and asks to see Luna.

At her name the girls start. There falls one of those unnatural silences that sometimes occurs even in a bustling hall of many conversations.

The man must not have passed through Smithton since last winter. The girls look spooked, and I am wondering if I should go over to the man and explain, when I see that Madame has gotten to him first. She pulls him aside, and she must whisper some milder, partial version of the truth, because he does not frown. Instead he soon goes upstairs with Coral. Madame's glare reprimands the remaining girls, who one by one focus again on their guests.

Before Madame's eyes can reach me, I have

turned back to the General. My hand unsteady, I pour us each another glass of wine.

The General always rises early. A mercy.

He departs, and I tell Millie to have Joanna prepare water for me. A quarter hour later I am tying up my hair and walking down to the chamber where we bathe: hot water steaming in the big wooden tub, dried petals floating on the surface, and a soft sheet waiting to dry me. I step in and let the water lull me into a stupor.

Last night, after my business with the General, I dreamed again. This time Luna and I were hanging laundry together in the courtyard, like sisters, or servants. She told me the story of how she came to be at Madame's and then she asked me mine.

It was too late now, but I wish we had told each other our stories. Instead she and I had talked of other things: about getting away and seeing more of the world.

"Wouldn't you like to see Saleekia?" she used to ask. "Everyone says it's beautiful there! We should go."

We never talked about how that could happen, though.

Near the end she had spoken of another plan: getting a rich nobleman to start her with his Players as an actress. "He'll have a brother or a friend who would be perfect for you. They'll come to take us away, and then," her lips used to curl into a smile, imagining it, "I'll tell Madame exactly how she can go fuck herself."

Luna expressed these dreams of hers as lightly as any other unreachable desire— like to drink all the spiced wine she wanted without the headache that followed; or to sleep a week of nights to herself; or to have everything she'd ever earned without Madame taking a share.

Madame never gave any sign she suspected what Luna thought of her, so I believe Luna actually *could* have made a good actress.

I'm unsure how long I've been there in the water, or even all that I have been thinking of, when there is a knock on the heavy door.

I call out, "Yes?" and it is Madame's own voice that murmurs. She tells me to come see her when I am done, and I wonder why she has come to tell me this herself, rather than sending Kate or Joanna; and then I wonder why she has bothered to tell me this at all, as I always pay her a visit in the morning. But by the next moment I understand that the unfamiliar note I heard in her voice was relief, and then I understand, too, why she knocked herself.

The water is cold, I realize. I climb out and call Millie to help me dress, then bring myself to Madame. She is at her breakfast, the account book open beside her plate.

"How was the General?" she asks.

He was as foul as ever, but I betray no complaints, and this pleases Madame. "Your discretion is a credit to you, Rose," she says.

"Thank you."

She writes a figure in her book. Sensing I have been dismissed, I turn to go. But she stops me after two steps.

"Rose?"

"Yes?"

"When the other girls are not around, you may call me May."

I give a small bow and leave her to her business, and we say nothing about Luna, or last night.

May's proffered intimacy takes me aback, though I have been at the House the longest of all the girls now, and though she has occasionally spoken candidly with me about business.

There was a rainy afternoon a couple months ago. Madame invited me into her office to share a cup of tea. She was unusually talkative. She talked about how things had been when she started working, and how she built her business, and some of the people she'd met over the years. Then she spoke about how the House was today, assessing her girls' different charms and talents: Lily has her lute and plays passing well, while Ruby has the best figure. But Ivy can make men laugh—every man she drinks with is convinced he's having a wonderful time.

"And me?" I asked Madame, unable to resist.

"You have mystery," she said. "That's your allure."

I laughed, thinking of my common origins, but I was enjoying being in her confidence. After Luna left, I hadn't gotten close to any of the newer girls. It had been a while since I'd had anyone to speak with.

When I first came to the House, I'd felt such fear of Madame. Naturally—I had no other place to turn, and I depended on her for everything. Even still I am in awe of her. As I've learned this trade, I've observed her ability to bend men's wills. I admire how persuasive she is and what a good negotiator. I see how she is respected and how her word is obeyed, and I am struck by how beautiful she is. With status she has found some kind of attraction more lasting than skin's.

Having no lord to answer to, she is more powerful than any noblewoman. She is wholly her own. And there is something quite appealing in that.

It's what Luna wanted for herself. Lately I, too, have been wondering what that would be like.

February comes, gray and dreary. Snow covers the fields and tents outside the city walls; it obscures the roads, too, along which fewer travelers come.

The cold whiteness outlines the branches of the plants in the courtyard and settles on the sill outside my window. Below me, a maid is sweeping the pathways clear for Madame's guests.

At the house next door, a cat waits, compact, hoping someone will let it in. And perhaps someone will: the jeweler's daughter has friends visiting, boys and girls. Their chatter and laughter spill out of the home and into our courtyard. I listen to it, remembering silliness, and lightheartedness, and warmth.

Dusk falls, and next door the guests leave, all but one, a boy. I have seen this boy before, lingering outside the girl's door—seen, too, how she waits to speak with him more, and alone, before stepping back into her father's shop.

She is fifteen, I think, and the boy about the same. Their eyes are shy. The dance between them is so beautifully awkward, so unsure and guiltless.

I remember those untamed marches between childhood and adulthood: territory too quickly conquered.

I close the shutter, step away from the window, and prepare for my night.

Most of the Wahnese forces go farther east to clear the countryside of rebels, so business in the hall slows a little. Still, Madame's House has a wide reputation and loyal clientele.

One night I entertain a merchant from Loq.

He's old, but I don't mind; these days I find myself relieved to have an uncomplicated man with simple needs. We do our business, and he asks me to speak to Madame about whether he might supply her. "What does she pay now for cloth of gold?" he mumbles, before sleep overtakes him.

Another night it is Master Arthur from Oakton, a town between Qwel and Loq. A funny little man, lonely, who talks and talks. He will have a wife and family some day, he tells me, and then he will give up Houses and Pretty Ladies. We will see, I think.

I add their coins to Madame's coffers, and other men's. Then it happens for the first time.

I am with a duke from Sidon, he laboring to take his pleasure. *This is not me, I am not here*, I hear myself thinking, as usual. But on this night for some reason, I can feel hot hands chaffing my skin everywhere they touch. I am aware of a mouth smothering my own, and I can't slip myself away from this body.

Like that, my spell is gone, the words ineffectual. Because I don't believe myself anymore: I realize I *am* here, in this place.

And I have been, all these thousand miserable nights.

It's midday before I come downstairs, and so the other Ladies are out of bed. Still in their robes, they slump and loll in their chairs in the informal way May doesn't allow when guests are present.

"Rose, how late you slept!" a voice calls. "And you look pale. Are you ill?"

I know I look poorly. I was unable to sleep. I just want to get to Harry, the cook, and ask him for some broth, then be by myself.

But Lily, who spoke, doesn't really care how I

am. When Madame gave the General to me back in December, Lily hoped it was a sign I was losing my rank. She thinks she deserves the Rose title by her higher birth—as if that made any difference now between us and what we do.

When I do surrender my title, it won't be to Lily. In bed I hear she gets the job done as well as any, but her main appeal is her harp-playing. She has the nimble, strong fingers for it. More importantly, she grew up with music-masters. (She spoke of her teacher once, and too affectionately—she was first plucked by him, I'd wager on it.) No matter how many lessons Madame arranges, it's too late for us village girls to be any good—at that, at least.

"I have some make-up you could use tonight," she offers. "You must be careful you don't lose that bloom, you know."

I stop beside her chair and lean to her ear, but I make sure my whisper is loud enough for the other girls to hear: "And *you* should be careful Madame doesn't catch you with the butcher. She doesn't value girls who devalue themselves."

Lily blushes crimson. She did not know that I know this, but she understands that this violation of Madame's rules could ruin her. She retreats with Ivy and Columbine, and I walk on to the kitchen, alone.

March arrives, and still I am having trouble sleeping. I start to crave rest the way some older Pretty Ladies crave wine, turning so fat and red-faced that their Madames kick them out of their Houses.

At night, I listen to the steady rhythm of the breath of whatever man is beside me. I hate them for their quick slide to their own tranquility after our business is through. I hear every rattling snore, every creak of the bed frame, and the bark and howl of every dog in the city. I am so exhausted that tears trail to my pillow, but still sleep doesn't come. I have lost it.

I've lost my forgetting, as well. Lying in the lonely dark, staring at the ceiling beams, I remember the lullaby my mother used to sing me; and the feel of peas in my hands, slipping from their pods; and the sweet words a boy used to whisper in my ear. All things better left forgotten.

Sometimes I hear Luna calling me. Sometimes I even think I see her, pale like her namesake. In these waking deliriums, she's as beautiful as she ever was and she seems happy enough. She asks me why I haven't come after her, and I don't know what to answer.

In nights' darkest hours, when it seems rest will never belong to me again, I fantasize about sleeping forever. What a paradise that would be! I could truly be alone, and my own: no one snoring beside me or laying over me; no light piercing my eye at just the moment my body finally finds peace.

After an eternity, eventually the night dies. The room lightens—so slowly, so gradually—and the servants downstairs begin to stir. My bedfellow snorts awake and leaves, and I get myself up, more exhausted and delirious than when I lay down, and stumble through my day, until the next night comes.

One night in the hall I jump as if something expensive had dropped and broken: I was sure I'd heard Luna's laugh, clear and light. I even turn around to look for her, but of course she is not there.

It takes me a moment to realize that it was *I* who had laughed, and that I was laughing still. And it makes me afraid that I did not realize this.

Spring advances on Smithton. Rain washes away the snow and softens the ground, and every day is lighter and warmer than the last.

Indeed, this morning my room feels stifling, or perhaps I am feverish. Tired of sitting at my window, I make myself go down to the garden. I think I have been inside too long; I should walk a little in the fresh air.

After so many overcast days, the cool brightness of the day feels harsh on my eyes. I walk a few steps with my eyes closed, protecting them from the glare. It's windy, too, and my hair flies about, lashing my face. I should go back inside for a ribbon so Millie won't have tangles to work out tonight, but after finally making myself come down here, I lack the will to return.

I pace patterns around and between the flower beds, mindless circles and eights. There is almost nothing to look at. The gardeners have raked away last year's leaves. The flower beds are bare-earth dark and naked, except for one eager sprout that pierces a brown leaf. The leaf, like a spitted fish over a campfire, is trapped there; it cannot blow away. And yet, it is curious: somehow the unfurling growth will eventually escape, the way a locust pulls itself out of its strange shell.

My head aches, and I pull my shawl around myself. I used to look forward to spotting the first crocus, to watching sprays of forsythia erupt. Now I'm impatient with the spring, ready for it to be summer already. Every year I've been at Madame's, I've fallen ill around this time.

A lizard skitters across the path in front of me, and then the cat that I always see around the neighbor's house. That's what draws my eyes to the ground, to the tuft of fluff, brown and white. I crouch to see.

A hatchling, hardly bigger than my thumb. I see the unsteady nest it must have fallen from. I look at the delicate down and baby feathers, at the little legs like twigs. So slight, so broken. I touch him gently, but he doesn't move.

My eyes fill, and I feel a familiar heaviness inside me. It isn't right, in spring, for something so small, so innocent–

The dead chick is light in my hand, like a piece of bread without crust. I can't bear the thought of the cat finding it. I kneel by one of the flower beds and scrape aside some soil, loose from the gardeners turning it. I remember the feel of earth on my hands—I used to help Mother with our garden.

I set the bird in the hole and cover it. I think I am crying. I know that I should get back to my room before anyone sees me here this way, but sadness paralyzes me. For a long time, I pat and smooth the earth.

I feel a presence standing over me, a straight figure blocking the light.

Madame. She *tsk*s me.

Sheepish, I stand and try to dust off my hands.

Madame looks disapprovingly at my ruined dress. She reaches for my wrists, observing the dust that fills the creases of my palms and cakes around my nails.

"Men pay a lot for these soft hands. You know that."

Last week when the physician made his monthly visit, he told Madame my body is healthy. But she misses little. She has been watching me in the hall, and she can tell my eyes are dark. I don't know how to explain what is wrong with me, or what I was doing. I don't know how to say that forgetting does not work for me anymore.

She looks at the state of me, my hair and my tears. Then it seems Madame remembers it's spring, and what that means for me; for when she tells me "Go inside and wash," it is with a softer tone.

It was spring when I first came to Madame's.

I was close to failing from hunger by the time I reached Smithton. In five days and through a score of villages, no passerby had given me so much as a penny or any more than a crust.

I had gone first to the church, but the priest chased me away, calling me the name of what I was not yet but what I'd soon become.

I was sitting against a courthouse wall, sniffling, when Madame's shadow fell on me. She bent down, and her thumb and forefinger locked on my chin, turning my face toward the weak spring sun. Despite the layers of dirt on me, she must have found some harmony in my features. In that voice that is not to be disobeyed, she told me to stand. I stood. With a practiced eye she assessed my form under my clothes, made her decision.

"You're too pretty to be out here. Come with me," she said briskly.

I had nothing. I was exhausted and friendless. She smelled like a garden and was the first person in a week to be kind to me, so I followed her.

The size of her home (for so I, naïve, at first thought it was) astonished me. Servants opened the door for her and called her Madame. She took off a cloak, revealing an elegant dress, and told a girl to bring me food; and I ate at the great table in the empty hall—roast chicken, bread (*white* bread!), cheese *and* fruit.

Eventually I noticed the paintings on the walls. They brought a hot blush to my cheeks, but I made no effort to leave when I realized where I was and who were the finely-dressed, unsmiling women looking over the balcony railing at me.

When I finished eating, Madame took me to a small room with a great tub and called for hot water. Before then, I'd only ever bathed in the cold creek. With her own hands, gentle as a mother, she put off my rags and washed my wretched limbs. And just as she had told each girl before, she told me how it would be.

I agreed to everything, no other idea of what to do. And then she summoned the old midwife to clean the rest of me, for she knew that part of the story without even asking.

My mother cast me out for the same reason village and city mothers do. Perhaps eventually she would have taken me back, remembering—shame to her or no shame—that she *did* love me. As it happened, I couldn't wait for her to remember.

But I left my mother's house easy-hearted. I was so certain of my Billy that I didn't care about her pious banishing. I thought that he would be my refuge and that we would make a home, without any help from my family or our judgmental neighbors.

I was so young.

Yet I *knew* Billy loved me. And so I went to him, told him that we were going to have a child. And there *was* joy on his face when he heard the news. He wanted to marry me, but he was afraid: "Father will never agree." For Master William had chosen another girl for his son—a well-to-do merchant's daughter, since little Billy had no talent for his father's ironwork.

I urged Billy to go to his father and stand up

for us. The engagement could be broken—such things happened all the time. But he was reluctant, and I didn't understand his reluctance.

He went to Master William, finally.

When Billy and I met again later that evening, I was eager to know what his father had said, but I set aside my impatience when I saw the state of Billy.

"What happened to you?" I asked, touching his bruised eye with light fingertips.

He said he'd walked into a branch in Cooper's Wood on the way to his father's. Billy'd always been clumsy, I thought. I lay a soft kiss on the swelling lid and stroked his black hair.

"Well, what did he say?"

He didn't want to tell me but finally did. Billy had made the case, but his father would not give his consent.

I admit I got impatient with Billy. Sometimes he didn't assert himself as I thought he ought. I suggested we go together to speak to Master William, but Billy was against the idea.

I got angry then. I didn't understand yet why Billy was so afraid, or why he wasn't bold enough to defy his father—hadn't I just defied my mother for *him*? That night, curled together under our pear tree, Billy promised we would think of something to do, but I suspected I would have to think for the both of us. That's how it usually was, with Billy and me.

I decided to go to Master William by myself in the morning. I didn't tell Billy what I planned, though. I had so much faith in my sincerity! I thought if Billy's father just understood that we loved each other, he wouldn't stand in our way. I would explain it right. So when Billy went to gather some eggs for our breakfast, I slipped off to the smithy.

Standing at the door of the shop, I had to shout to get Master William's attention. He let go of his bellows to hear me. He was sweaty and sooty already.

I had prepared my speech the night before, and I knew it by heart: I told him that I loved Billy and that we were going to have a child. That Billy was happy with me, and didn't he want his son to be happy? And didn't he remember being young once?

Billy's father listened as I said all these things. His face was unreadable to me. I knew nothing about men then, and (of course) I had misjudged this man. He felt no pity, only violence and lust, and there I was, alone like a fool.

He grabbed my wrist, leering. "I know what you are."

When I recoiled, he sneered and said something about my vanity, promising to show me his "fires" hadn't "faded." It didn't matter to him that his son had had me, or that I was with child. It didn't matter that I screamed and clawed. He was a big man. Strong, as smiths are.

It felt like I was there and not there, at the same time. I remember I could see myself pressed into the dirt of his shop floor. I realize I shouldn't have been able to see myself under him like that, but somehow I could—as if I were a cat hiding in the rafters above, looking down, unperturbed. As if that were not me, there.

When he was done, he dusted dirt from his knees and rose. He tugged his leather apron back in place and told me to go away and have my bastard. He said that if I knew what was good for me, I would leave his boy alone to the good future he'd prepared for him. He said no one would believe me if I talked, anyway.

I struggled to breathe and find the pieces of

myself. I didn't understand what had just happened. It could not have been my skirt that he had yanked up; it was not my mouth he had held down with his calloused palm; not me, who he had forced his way inside.

And so it didn't seem like my hand that reached for, and found, some tool propped against the stone wall: long when it swung, and heavy when it struck Master William's head, like a shovel breaks a clod.

Somehow, I don't remember it, I left the smithy and got back to our meeting place. Billy was gone. I sat small against our tree, the bark hard against my back. I don't know how long I sat there, but I knew Billy would return, eventually.

He did, hours later. Pale and quiet, he asked if I knew what had happened at his father's place. When I told him, my torn clothes and bruises my witnesses, he said I was lying—his father hadn't. Wouldn't.

I was crying, begging Billy to come away with me, to take care of me. He cried and flailed for his dead father, but he wouldn't let me touch him, and he didn't cry for me or our child.

He ran away from me. I waited as long as I could but he didn't return, so I left our village before the next sunrise. If he watched me go, he must not have told the sheriff which direction I went. I never saw Billy again, or my mother.

Our child would have turned three last December, had he lived. I don't know why but I think it was a boy. Too young, too unformed to tell, the midwife who worked for Madame that spring had said.

That is how I came to be at Madame's. That is the story I had to tell, if anyone would ask.

April comes. For months snow and rain have soaked in the ground where the Wahnese and Qwelli fought, leveling it. Grass covers the field now. From my window I can't tell where they dug the graves.

The porters light the lanterns later each evening. The maids have taken the heaviest blankets off our beds, and they build smaller fires.

The Wahnese have started returning to Smithton, so tonight we have a fair number of guests. One by one the men who have money to spend go upstairs, and the poorer ones go home for the night.

I am still downstairs when Lily goes up with a client. She smirks and gloats that I remain below, yet unchosen.

An hour later, all the men have left. Kate and Millie extinguish the candles and push the benches back in place, and I go to my room, alone.

I push open the shutter and lean my head against the window frame. I can see nothing, but still my eyes are looking east, toward the road that brought me here. I think of the girl in the fairy tale who leaves a trail of crumbs so she can find her way out of the forest; and then I think of a trail like that between here and my village, five days' walk away, but with pieces of myself left along the way.

I go to my dressing table, take my hair down and brush it out, more than it needs. I feel dull and ugly, and I am so weary. I should be grateful for an unexpected night to rest unmolested, but these days I am reluctant to lie down. When my work was done and on my nights off, I used to rest well—used to have beautiful, dreamless sleep, oblivion. Now I have trouble getting to sleep almost every night. And when I finally do sleep, I dream. I've come to hate every goose-down-stuffed inch of this bed, every thread of its soft linen, every twist of the ropes in its frame.

I wonder if I should worry that I have been passed over. Madame's good-night to me, at least, betrayed no reproach: "It's how the business goes," she shrugged.

Still, my pride smarts.

There was a time, not long ago, when I triumphed for signs of these men's adoration—when I strove to gain, and then to keep, the title "Rose." To think *me*, a village girl, called "my lady" and given gifts by dukes and nobles! Before I came to Smithton I'd never held two pennies together, much less felt the weight of gold (or other things) in my palm.

Billy and I'd never had a bed, nothing softer than the sprung grass.

I can admit that when I first began working, I would sometimes feel something not unpleasant, despite myself. Sometimes back then I even let myself imagine it was Billy with me on this luxurious bed—his hands, his hair, his mouth—

Soon enough I realized it was better to forget all that.

You see, it didn't take long for me to realize that my nights at Madame's were more like that afternoon in the smithy than any afternoon under the pear tree. But until tonight, I didn't realize how dangerous a pleasure it is to wield power over these men, and how fleeting.

Luna must have realized this. She had been here six years, to my now-four. I look at myself in the mirror on my dressing table, and I know I cannot do this forever. My old incantation has not worked for weeks—no, months—because I know, and because I cannot pretend not to anymore, that this *is* me, and I *am* here; and I don't want to be either. I want to find the pieces of myself, or I want to be somewhere else, and someone else. Someone who is not the one told what to do, for a change.

Some girls go on, like Madame did, to run a House, or at least a brothel. That's one way out.

There are other ways. A few girls mistress up: besot a fool sufficiently to secure a household of their own, no longer Madame's to keep. A man pays a high cost to buy her if she's still young and pretty, far less if she's past her prime. This is perhaps the best bet for leaving, and I *have* thought about cultivating someone, making some man want to rescue me. I have enough allure for that, I think. But in a town the size of Smithton, there are few prospects. Last fall a wool merchant passing through asked me to go with him to Hillstead. I scoffed, because Hillstead is a nowhere-village where it wouldn't do to get abandoned. But now I wonder why I didn't say *yes*; I could have been *not-me* there as easily as here.

Under a brick in the courtyard I have a small, hidden stash—second-rate jewels that men have given me and a few coins I've held back from Madame. I'm not so foolish as to think these would be enough to escape with, though. And if I were to fail, there would be no coming back. Last year a girl called Daisy ran away from the House. She was pretty and seemed sweet-natured, though I really couldn't say; she was only here a fortnight before she left. A week later, she knocked on our door, alone again and contrite. But Madame wouldn't have her back. Made quite a scene, in fact, for the sake of the other girls. She demanded Daisy hand over her dress (Madame had given it to her) and left the girl standing in the courtyard in nothing but a thin shift. Coral says she heard Daisy ended up at the stable at the Golden Lute. If that's true, she's working a lot harder for a lot less than we have from Madame.

Then there's the way Luna left the House, and this work: white sheet wrapped around her white body. The morning we watched them lift her out of the pink-watered bath, her arms looked like scarlet ribbons. I saw that, but not where they buried her. The priest (that same damned priest who gave me only a chastening glance and his unkind words) wouldn't give Luna rest in the churchyard, nor would Madame allow us to follow the steward outside the city walls to see where he laid her.

After that Madame no longer allowed us to bar the door when we bathed, and she started counting and locking away the knives each night.

Midsummer comes with its long days and short nights. It's been half a year since the foreigners won Smithton, and the cost of bread is back to what it was before they came. The rest of the Wahnese have returned from their campaigns. I've watched them setting up their tents outside the walls. The officers have been returning to Madame's hall, which is crowded again.

Upstairs our maids are finishing our hair and make-up. Downstairs the porter will be setting the tables.

I am rearranging the combs in my hair when Millie brings me word: I've been requested by a guest. He will have his supper first, and I should wait for him in my room.

I freshen my perfume, see that the candles are arranged correctly, and wait. It's a warm, quiet night until the music begins in the hall. Then the laughter grows louder as Madame's guests imbibe.

My guest tonight could be the equivalent of the General, but I don't care. I'm relieved not to have to go downstairs, to smile and flirt for the whole room.

An hour passes. When the man opens the door, I smell a smell like a cut meadow after rain has spoiled the hay. He has washed away the road dirt and is wearing one of the fine robes Madame provides her guests.

I recognize him, actually: it's the young prince who visited me the night of the Qwelli defeat, before all my restlessness began.

I want to resent him for that. At the time I blamed him for carrying so much sadness with him. But now (and it surprises me to realize this) I find I'm glad to see that the somber boy has not gotten himself killed.

He places his coin on the table (it is gold—generous), and I greet him with a kiss, which he returns.

After a moment, though, he stops: "What's this? Where is your cruelty, my lady?"

I lean back a little but hold his eyes—the gray I remember, but they are no longer shy. "Do you want me to be cruel, my lord?"

"You were cruel the first time I visited you."

"Did you visit before? And was I cruel?" I smile, pretending not to remember. "Many of Madame's guests like that. But if I was cruel, either you like that, or you have forgiven me the abuse, for you are here now."

"I take no pleasure in cruelty."

"Then I will have to be amusing," I smile, stepping away from him. He is more handsome than I remember, and I feel strangely lighthearted.

But he shakes his head. "It's not amusement

that I need."

I sit, pat the mattress. "A soft bed, then?"

When he smiles, I realize I have given away too much: he knows that I remember him and how much more greedily he looked at my bed than at me. But he doesn't triumph to have caught me out. Instead he banters like an experienced guest: "Yes, a soft bed… with soft pillows to lie upon."

I had heard the Wahnese army got as far east as Loq. I am thinking of the Houses that he must have visited since I saw him. Madame speaks approvingly of them. Indeed, the prince has become less callow: he has the fluent grace of a man who has done this many, many times.

He has not joined me yet, so I lean back, regarding him. "You look well."

"As do you."

"You've seen more fighting since you visited us."

"Yes."

"Were you afraid?"

"Only fools are not."

I hold silent, but he goes on as if he heard the retort I'd merely thought: "And no, lady, I'm not a fool. Or, at least—I'm becoming less of one than I used to be."

Music from downstairs rises up. Mirth we're not party to.

He turns to the window. He is looking toward the field that was bloody when he was last here, so I am able to steal a long glance of him. At first I thought he looked older, but it is only the confidence that he now wears. He is still sad, only he hides his grief better than he did then.

His eyes remain on the dark field beyond the walls. "When I first rode out," he says, "I thought I wanted to die."

I swallow, thinking of my recent, dark dreams of Luna, and how I'd found myself testing a knife's edge with my thumb.

"I realized I was wrong about that," he says. He turns and looks back at me, those eyes so sad but calm, and I realize at last that I won't choose Luna's way out.

He says, "It's difficult sometimes to know what we want."

I can't say anything to this. Not knowing what they wanted was a problem only nobles had, I thought. I was a Pretty Lady: it was not for me to want. There wasn't any use in it. *You can wish for a peach in winter,* my mother used to say, *but it can't be had.*

"Do you know what you want right now?" I tilt my face to his in a manner that tends to get a response from men.

He kisses me again.

When we lay down, he closes his eyes like I did when I was new here: like he needs to leave aside memories and body and self, as if there's no other way to escape. Other men's moments with me are about blood and heart and lust, rush and thrill and release. But for this one it seems about *not* feeling, for a while; it's about oblivion.

He is passionate but gentle, and I think he must not be a bad man. I feel guilty that I teased him so much that night, months ago. Tonight I want to make his forgetting last as long as I can. I want to be kind: to take him back to his past, his hopes and dreams, at least for a while.

And I do. He is with me, and I am with him; and I hear none of the noise downstairs, for I have taken him—us—far away. So far I almost lose myself there. For a moment I forget I am at Madame's, forget

I am unhappy, forget he is a prince.

After he comes, I lie quiet and still so that whatever fantasy he is visiting can live on a little longer. Gradually my heart slows, and my breathing. He is stroking my breast absently, and I am caressing my own illusions. Only when I open my eyes do I realize I've been holding them shut.

It is too short a time. A different tremor passes through him, soft as a new soul quickening in a womb, and he sighs. Remembering has returned.

I feel the retreat of his hand from my skin—the warm spot where it had rested, turning cold—and he rolls away from me, but he arranges my arm to rest across him, and then the blanket to cover us both. He falls into a quiet sleep. Eventually I do, too.

I intended to be more mannerly the next morning than I'd been on his first visit, but that night I slept more soundly than I had in quite some time. When I open my eyes, he's already dressed.

"I didn't mean to wake you," he says.

I rise and pull on my robe to see him to the chamber door.

It has rained overnight. Perhaps that is why I rested so well—the peaceful sound. But it's a damp morning.

I must have shivered, for the prince reaches out and pulls my robe tighter about me. He arranges my hair outside the neck of the gown before kissing my cheek and saying farewell—as if the robe were a cloak, and I his cousin, and this a friendly parting on the threshold of some fine manor.

He closes the door quietly, and I see he's left a noble-sized tip on the table, next to last night's coin.

Madame is (as is her habit) at her accounts.

I wait for her to look up, and when she does, I hand her the prince's coins.

Her eyes' glint matches the pieces'. The creases of her face arrange themselves into a smile. "The Wahnese prince. He remembered you—asked for you."

Impressed, she is recalculating my value. Many of the officers have taken on regular girls for the remainder of their encampment. She pauses, deciding.

"You're to be available whenever he calls. That means tonight you're restricted to dancing and playing cards, in case he visits. We'll see if we can interest him in an arrangement."

I find I'm not upset by this. I don't mind the prince or the idea of being his exclusively.

Millie finds me downstairs and hands me my potion. I take it to the window to sip, lingering downstairs on purpose. I want to see Lily's face when she hears the news.

That night, the hall full and all the girls busy, a Rhudian ambassador is eyeing me, but Madame has the steward explain that I am not available. I am a baited hook, awaiting a bigger fish.

The air is changed after last night's rain. A breeze enters the shutters and I feel strangely free. This night I am like a guest, pleasing myself. I take seconds at dinner and sip Madame's good wine—not to be drunk, but to savor the smooth warmth. I flirt and dance until my heart is pounding and I feel giddy and dizzy.

At the end of the night, my body tired but content, I go upstairs. While others work, I sleep soundly, and alone.

The tap on my door comes the next day.

"Come in," I say, expecting Millie. But it is May.

She has spoken to the prince and they have come to terms. He will visit a few times a week. Madame will not give me any other clients, not even on the nights when he does not visit.

"And he is not interested in seeing any of the other girls," she adds.

I show that I take this as the compliment she means it to be.

She is carrying a bundle with her. She hands it to me. "I want you to have this. It was Beth's—my daughter's," she adds, and her usual poise is a little off, like a lace that has skipped one eyelet.

Luna had told me the story: May planned to leave the House to her daughter, but the girl had died in the last plague outbreak ten years back.

I unfold the cloth carefully. It's an elaborate gown, red as wine, heavy with embroidery and braid. It is worth a ransom.

"It's beautiful."

May holds the dress against me, evaluating how the color and fit will suit me. She nods her approval. "You're taller than she was," she says quietly. "But Millie can let out the hem."

"Thank you, May," I begin, but she calls Millie and leaves before I can say anything else.

That night I prepare with care—Madame's dress, adjusted to fit me; a ring another prince gave her long ago; and a necklace some spendthrift merchant gave to me.

After dinner the prince comes to my room. He embraces me right away, setting a kiss in the valley between my breasts, just beneath the merchant's pendant.

I laugh and step back—suddenly nervous, I don't know why. I reach for the wine pitcher and glasses. "Have a drink with me, your highness."

He shakes his head, though. "No, I thank you. But you go ahead, my lady."

I set the pitcher down, protesting; it would be unmannerly for me to drink alone.

He hesitates. "A moment, then," he says. He goes to the door, calls his servant, and whispers instructions. The man returns with a new bottle of wine, which the prince opens and pours himself.

"To you," he says, and we drink. But I am curious about who it is he doesn't trust—me, Pretty Ladies in general, Madame, or the Qwelli.

I endeavor to be light and cheerful: "I'm honored you chose me and not another of Madame's girls."

He shifts a little. He heard the question I have not quite asked. The prince pauses. "You want to know why you."

Indeed, I do; I want him to talk a little, to compliment me. But his face has become sober. I fear I've offended him somehow.

He says, "Do you need flattery, my lady?"

I find myself blushing. He rejected my flattery, his first night here. "I— No. No, I don't."

He sets down his wine and touches my free hand—an apology for his tone. He is not angry.

"Let's not deceive ourselves," he says. I nod, agreeing. And after that exchange, I do not try again to make him talk.

I understand what I do for the prince: help him forget. Not forever, but for a time. He seems grateful that I understand this.

He is neither demanding nor cruel. With him, it is never as it was in the smithy. Nor is it as it was under the pear tree. But it is not unpleasant. He is not unkind.

Lily resented me for a while, but she soon has her own reason to gloat: when Lord Galen hires girls for a feast at his estate, he requests Lily to be his personal companion.

Madame has arrangements with a handful of the local nobility. Sometimes when a lord is entertaining guests at his home, girls are allowed to leave the House and attend. And this gathering of Galen's was to be very large. In fact, the hall would close, as it does only a handful of nights a year, because all the girls would be needed there.

All except me, that is. By the terms of Madame's arrangement with the Wahnese prince, I was not to accept other work.

With her Ladies gainfully disposed of, and free from running the House for the night, Madame decided she would visit Qwel. She'd been negotiating with the proprietress of a House there, she confided to me, thinking about taking on a new girl. She wants me to fill in for her in her absence: to receive deliveries to the House, escort the girls to and from Galen's estate, and prepare the hall to reopen the next night.

I'm not completely surprised May has asked me to do this. I've begun to suspect she intends to train me in the business, maybe even sell the House to me when she cannot manage it anymore.

And I admit: I am curious about how it would feel to command.

Madame leaves early, after giving me final instructions: "See that Coral knows she's not to drink too much—you know how she gets."

I spend the morning in May's pretty sitting room, signing off on deliveries. After lunch is served and the maids have finished helping the Ladies dress, I call the servants together to dismiss them and tell them when to return.

Then I go to the Great Hall, where the Ladies are gathered and waiting for me. They are decked in Madame's finest, and they have been giggling and admiring each other's attire. But when I enter, they straighten up and fall silent like they do for Madame.

I look them over, checking that they have prepared with sufficient care. They are mostly silent for this, but Ruby does ask, tentative: "Lady Rose, why did Madame go to Qwel?"

Lily follows Ruby's question with a bolder one: "Is she looking for another girl?"

I give Lily a cool look and evasive answer: "That's Madame's business."

Ivy starts to babble about how she will not share her maid with anyone else, and that leads Columbine to renew an old bicker over which of them holds precedence over the other.

"Girls!" They fall silent and look chastened at the sharp note in my voice, and I am pleasantly surprised.

The estate is a mile south of the city gates. We set out on foot rather than in carriages. In this way we are a walking declaration for the quality and elegance of Madame's House.

The girls have fear enough of Madame that I have no problems from them as we process. Indeed, they know how to behave: how to hold themselves in their finery, how to pretend not to note the gapes and stares. Young guards at the gate who have been horsing around with one another fall silent when we pass.

Walking in front of the group, I can almost imagine I am alone. From my window, this road outside the walls looks so smooth. It is different when you are on it. White pebbles stand out bright against dull ones in the road. When I was a girl, I used to collect them. A part of me is tempted to pick one up now, feel its shape against my thumb, but this is not how I must behave.

We arrive at Lord Galen's and the steward gives us entrance to his Great Hall, which is decked with greenery for the feast. The girls who have never left the House gawk at the wealth until Lord Galen joins us.

"A pleasure to see you, Lady Rose." He bows, kissing my hand like he does Madame's, then looks admiringly over the girls. Galen is light on his feet tonight, feeling festive. I know his moods well: he used to visit me when I first arrived at Madame's. But he never stays content with any one girl. For him it is all about the unknown and the new.

We arrange when I will call for the girls the next afternoon, and I take my leave.

We are not often outside the city walls—not often outside our House's walls, frankly. It feels good to walk freely. Of late, Madame has been giving me this privilege more often. Today, without Madame to watch how long my errands take, I choose a longer way home, by a little farm set off the road. Iris pointed this place out to me last summer.

My steps slow, then stop. Down the tree-lined lane, I glimpse a blond head running after another child. The girl and the boy each have switches in their hand. It takes me a moment to realize that the blond head is Anne. Last summer she was still like a baby; now she is a little girl. Four, I think.

She resembles more each passing year that governor's son who used to visit Iris.

Naturally May must have firm rules: she loses a few months' earnings every time a morning potion fails. The maids must watch us drink them, to make sure no one forgets. May can't have Iris's situation look desirable to the others, either, and so Iris sees her daughter only when Madame permits it. Last summer was the last time.

I did not tell Iris I would be passing this way. I don't know if it will make her happy or sad to know that I saw Anne, who is prancing now, and the stick is a sword or a fishing pole, a whip or a scepter.

I have been stopped here for a while. I hadn't meant to be seen, but the girl spots me. She does not recognize me. Nevertheless, friendly and easy, she greets me. She waves with her whole arm, not quitting until I wave back.

I feel an aching pang, a bitter-sweetness when she returns to her games and her laughter. But she looks healthy. Happy. I will tell Iris so, if she wants to know.

Sweaty and hot from my walk, I re-enter the city. The back of my embroidered bodice scratches against my skin, and I am more than ready to take off these fine clothes and sit in my room with a glass of wine: no Madame, no Ladies, and no servants, and the prince not scheduled to visit until tomorrow night. What will it be like, I wonder, to read in peace while I eat my cold supper, and to go to bed in a quiet house?

I pass the jeweler's shop and come to Madame's courtyard, and that's when I see the girl sitting outside the House, on the step.

"Didn't you hear? You have the night off," I

call, thinking she is one of the girls who helps in the kitchen. Then she raises her head, and I realize I've never seen this girl before.

She stands, her eyes take in my low-cut gown and jewels, and I feel something like embarrassment.

"What do you want?" I ask, but already I know. Girls appear on Madame's doorstep a few times a year.

She starts to cry.

"You'd better come in," I say.

I usher her into Madame's office and shut the door, then pour some water for her. I am trying to think of what Madame did and said, what she would have me do.

The girl chokes a little as she drinks from Madame's fine wineglass. She's pretty, even in rags, and even though she's been sleeping outdoors for a few nights. She is struggling not to stare at the erotic sculptures that decorate the office.

She sets the glass down carefully. Straightens her back, takes a jerky breath. "My lady, I left home. I couldn't stay there. Could I... Would you not teach me to...?"

But she is so young she cannot even say what she is asking.

My eyes flit to her stomach. "Are you...?"

She shakes her head quickly. Not that, at least.

The girl before me is beautiful, even in tears. A true curse, that. I look at her soft curves and know she is just the sort of girl Madame would want to cultivate: gentle, compliant, unaware of her beauty. She would be a steady earner. Lily would hate her.

She starts to bite a nail, nervous, then stops herself. I think she must be no older than the jeweler's daughter next door.

"Listen to me carefully," I say, and it frightens me how much I sound like Madame: the steel in my voice despite my whisper, and the command in it to be obeyed. "You are going to leave here and go home. Find an aunt or a woman neighbor who has more pity than the ones you fled. You'll have to pretend not to hear what the others say about you. But don't stay here."

Madame will be furious with me if she learns. She's been looking for another girl, and I'm sure she would take this one in. But these words are a torrent from my mouth. They soak into the girl.

My voice softens, and it's as if I'm talking to myself: "It wasn't good where you come from, but it's worse here. You see that now, don't you?"

She doesn't argue. Instead she bursts into tears again, relieved I have decided this for her.

She has nothing, and no way back. I take an earring from my ear and set it in her palm, folding her fingers over it. I tell her not to accept less than ten. Then I tell her where she can take a meal and hire a ride back home.

She nods, mute, and disappears, like a mouse escaping a cat.

When she is gone, I don't know why, but I burst into tears myself.

The next afternoon I collect the girls from Lord Galen's. One of his cousins is saying good-bye to Iris, kissing her hand, promising to see her again soon.

When we're on the road to Smithton, Lily hands me the purse of coins the group has earned, but she gloats a while over the ring Galen gave to her personally. She shows it off to each of the others.

"Maybe he'll want an arrangement with you,"

Columbine suggests.

Lily shrugs as if it doesn't matter to her, but she isn't fooling anyone. Only after every girl has had her turn cooing does she pass the ring to me, looking for approval or awe.

It is a square green stone, pretty and bright. I say as much to her.

But I know there will be a flaw. When she gets permission from Madame to visit a jeweler, he will find the fleck that mars its brilliance.

She is content, though. "Lovely," I repeat, letting her have a few days' joy. It is little enough.

Madame returns and calls me to her room. I hang up her cloak and she hands me something wrapped in a napkin. "Here, taste this cake. I think I'll have Harry try to make it. What do you think?"

I take a bite. "It's good."

She sits at her dressing table and pulls off her riding gloves, then begins putting her jewelry away. "So—how was Lord Galen's?"

"Everything went well," I assure her. "And your journey, May?"

"Oh, the journey was fine. But Qwel—" She makes an exasperated sound. "No good. Buckteeth, can you imagine? It hasn't come to *that* yet."

She does not seem particularly worried. She has been in this business a long time. I wonder how many girls have slept in my room and thought of that window as theirs; I wonder how many have been called Rose.

"Lord Galen was very pleased, and Iris was much praised," I offer, explaining about Galen's cousin.

"Really?" May is surprised, but she nods after thinking about this. "Yes, she's in better looks than Lily, these days. Perhaps I'll do something for her." May points at the water pitcher: "Come here with that."

I pour the water for her and she washes her face and hands. I wait until she is drying them to say, "It's been a year since she saw Anne."

May's eyes darken and her voice hardens into a wall again. "No. That's not a good idea."

I put the pitcher back on its table and say nothing, but Madame sees something in my posture or expression. "What? You have something to say?"

"No, Madame, nothing."

I do not mention the girl who came.

The prince calls regularly, two or three times a week, and we do what we do. Occasionally he visits in the afternoon, and we are warm skin under cool sheets, waiting for a breeze to find the open window. But usually he arrives in the evening, after the day's heat has passed; it is pleasant then and cool, and we sleep comfortably the night afterwards.

I said at the first that he was not like other princes. After knowing him a little better, I think this still. He is neither vain nor extravagant, though he is generous enough. (Madame's coffers are richer, certainly, and I have secretly set aside a few more coins.)

But more than that: he seems different from other *men*. For instance, most love to speak about themselves, but this one is quiet. And most want to be in the hall with me for a few hours before retiring upstairs, to be seen by their friends and rivals. They pay a premium for my title and the message my beauty sends about *their* wealth and power.

This prince is not like that. Sometimes he asks me to dine with him in the hall, but most often he sends word that he'll meet me in my room.

The other men say he is a good soldier. Princes do not usually fight—command, yes, but not fight. By going to war, I wonder what he is trying to prove to his father, or his father to him.

I wonder what he was like as a boy.

I have spent another easy night with my prince. He leaves my room, and I cannot help it: I go to the window and peer around the curtain. He is crossing the courtyard and heading back for the camp. I watch him and his morning shadow: walking the same path, but at different angles.

I am ravenous this morning. I don't wait for Millie but rather go down to the kitchen to ask Harry, the cook, to make me an omelet.

Today he isn't alone. A child, hair as shiny and black as a crow wing, is with him. How odd it is, to see a child in the House! He is kneeling on a stool so he can look in the pot Harry stirs, and he is humming a song.

I remember this tune from long ago. I hum with the boy. He stops for a second but smiles at me, coy.

Then Harry turns, sees me, nods. I like Harry. Besides being a good cook, he never meddles with the girls. He's like a vintner untempted to drink; he has been married (he likes to boast) twelve years.

"'Morning, Harry. Who's this?" I ask, suspecting.

"My youngest, Tom. Say hello to Lady Rose," he prompts.

"Hullo, my lady," Tom chirps.

My hand is drawn to the boy's hair. It is straight as angry rain and sleek as duck feathers. A warmth passes through me.

The kitchen has never felt so bright, so welcoming. Harry's voice smiles when he asks what he can do for me.

I am about to ask for my breakfast and find an excuse to eat it here, rather than in my room as I typically do, when a commotion approaches from the passageway. Harry glances nervously in the direction of his son.

"Harry? Harry!"

It is Madame. As she does with all the servants, she has started commanding before she is in the room. Now she has entered, and she notices the child.

Harry wipes his hands on his apron. He whispers something to the boy, who climbs off his stool and creeps behind his father's leg.

May turns a piercing look to the cook. "You know the rules, Harry. This is unacceptable."

"I know, Madame, but today his mother had to—"

"I don't care for excuses, Harry."

He quickly surrenders. "No, ma'am."

"This will not happen again, or you will be leaving us. Understood?"

"Yes, ma'am."

She holds him over the spit with her gaze a moment longer, then returns to business, giving thorough instructions for supper. She ignores Tom.

"Yes, ma'am," Harry bows. "As you wish."

Madame turns to go, and her eyes sweep over me. She will be displeased if I stay. Wordlessly I take a piece of bread from the basket and leave, too.

She stops in the corridor to speak with me, muttering truisms about the need to be firm with employees.

"Yes, Madame," I agree.

She concludes her tirade with a compliment, unexpected: "You're looking yourself again. This spring, you were getting so thin."

"I- thank you, May. I am well," I say, steady as I can, and wonder what she is seeing that I cannot hide.

"From the prince." Millie sets a basket on the table. "He says he'll see you tonight instead of tomorrow."

Peaches. They are ripe and perfect, cleaner smelling than perfume. I laugh with pleasure like a child, unguarded and honest, and the sound feels strange in my ears.

"Leave me this one, then take the rest to share with the other Ladies," I say. "But take one for yourself, first."

Millie puts the fruit in her pocket, though she seems confused by my cheerfulness.

I'm confused, too. Why has this humble gift pleased me so? I think of my mother's saying, even if it is not winter but rather the season for peaches. There has been something in the corner of my mind, like the name of an acquaintance that must be summoned up, but I don't yet know what it is.

I start preparing for the prince. I pull a dress over my head and am smoothing the wrinkles of the fabric over my belly when I understand what I have been thinking of: just then, in that moment, I began to believe that it was possible for me to want something and to *have* it.

When Millie comes in to brush my hair, I am still adjusting to this new thought: for what *do* I want?

"Thank you—I can do the rest," I tell Millie.

When she is gone I set down my makeup and go to the window.

Sunset advances, gold and pink, and people

flood the city streets, returning to their homes and families. I imagine their work and homes and days: a nobleman passing by on a fine horse. The widow next door sweeping off her step. The peddler pushing home his cart.

And two young people—the jeweler's daughter and a boy—who walk slower than the crowd around them. They are finding the best way to fit their fingers together, and something is being made between them. I smile at the hopefulness, and the sweetness, and the trust of this fragile link.

Harry the cook is turning onto the lane in front of the House to come to work. Little Tom rides his father's shoulders, and a woman walks with them. I think she is Harry's wife, for she and Harry hold another child's hands. Harry pauses under a tree branch that hangs over the garden wall and Tom tries to grab at the leaves.

What *do* I want? To be Madame, to be rich and give commands? Or to be someone's mistress—the lady of some manor house? There is more freedom in that, without making others unfree.

Or am I wanting something else entirely?

I pull my arms around my middle, tight, the way the prince clutches me when he sleeps, and in the length of a breath I know; and it is so clear to me that I laugh again.

Yet a voice inside me tries to caution: *It's not for Pretty Ladies to want.*

—*But why not?* a defiant voice I used to know argues back. I could have desires, too, or again.

Not you. It's too late for you, the darkness says.

I hesitate, afraid. If I let myself hope for this and it does not come to pass, I'll feel even more alone than I was before. As alone as I was when Luna died.

It's such a difficult thing, reviving hope! First it must be untangled from memory, picked clean and free from hopes that have died. You have to become as open as a child again. You have to believe that there can be comfort and solace, relief and love—you have to trust that you can reach out and grasp them, and then hold them for a while.

For a moment I think of my poor sweet Billy, and of a flash of shining black hair, and of happiness and warmth: and I remember what it is to feel whole. Complete.

I can be that again.

The prince will be here soon. With care, I finish making myself ready for him.

He lingers in my bed this morning.

I like his breath on my neck, and this way he traces my hair around my ear. I know this mark on his upper arm, some scar from childhood, and this place on my breast where his palm always comes to rest. And I know the shudder of his body, and his knee and foot finding mine under the sheet.

He stretches and gets up, and it pleases me to watch him dress: the exact way he buckles his belt, and the order in which he pulls on his boots, always the same. When he is collecting himself to go, he runs his fingers through his hair, and it is as if his whole body sighs, even though he breathes steadily, when he finally stands.

Millie knocks after he has left. She has my morning potion on a tray. I have been waiting for this.

"Just leave it there on the table," I say. "I'm not done sleeping."

She hesitates. She's supposed to wait until I drink, then bring down the empty cup. She knows

Madame's rules. I do, too.

"Don't worry," I say, feigning a yawn. "I'll bring the cup to the scullery when I go downstairs."

Fear crosses her face—May has dismissed girls over more trivial infractions, and everyone has heard about the censuring Harry got for having Tom in the kitchen.

"You're busy, and I'm tired. Madame will never know." I wait. I am anxious but must not show it.

But my maid wants to like me these days and to stay on friendly terms. "Yes, Lady Rose," she says. Bowing, she leaves.

After that first morning, it is easy to convince her. And in this way, Millie and I set the pattern that I need in order to have what I want.

Sometimes before we lie down he asks me to read to him, or we play a hand of cards, or chess. I find myself enjoying these strangely normal pastimes, like we are friends.

He likes to win. Still, he warns me when I am about to make a blunder—gives me a chance to reconsider the play. Makes a little admiring sound when I find a good move.

After, when he kisses me, it feels fond. Like comfort, or the beginning of happiness.

One night in July it is too hot to sleep.

He is resting soundly. I rise and steal to the window to look out at the night, like I used to do when I was unhappy. But already I feel changed. Rather than looking for the road I walked here, I am imagining all the roads I cannot see and the distant places they carry you to.

I have been thinking about what it would be

like to be outside these walls and this city. I wonder what faraway Wahn is like: its neighborhoods and squares, and the riches it has brought home from all its conquests. What they eat and wear at the capital, and court, and how the children pass their holidays.

The prince's breathing alters and I realize he is awake. I know the feeling of his eyes on me.

I expect him to summon me to him like bedfellows usually do. Instead he climbs out and comes to me.

I shift over, sharing the open window with him. Silent, he stands beside me, looking at the hulking black shapes that are the city walls, and the emptiness that is the field where he fought last year.

He takes my hand in his. It is firm. Reassuring. I am glad it's dark and he cannot see how I flush at this intimacy. We stand there, alone together in the dark, and I feel something small and fragile inside me, like hope. Like wings.

It's afternoon, and the flowers I cut from the garden are strewn on a table in the hall. I am setting them in a vase. Tonight they will perfume my room for the prince's visit.

I used to bring my mother flowers from the meadow near Cooper's Wood. She would set them in a clay mug in the center of our table and they would nod between us as we ate. I remember the delight that filled her face when I handed them to her. I dreamed about this, last night.

Madame walks past me and my project, but a moment later she has returned, as if she has reconsidered something.

"Rose, about exclusive clients."

"Yes?" I stop humming to answer her. I hadn't

realized I was humming.

"They are still clients," she says.

I push a stem into the neck of the vase. Without looking up, I know May is staring at me, trying to see my thoughts.

"I know what that means," I tell her.

"Do you?"

"Yes." I look up, meet her eye. "This is business."

It's the right answer, but she is not sure she believes I mean it.

"If he asks, would you like to go with the prince? When he leaves Smithton?"

This would be her decision, not mine, the two of them negotiating the price of my freedom just as they negotiated the current arrangement between him and me.

"He has not asked," I tell her, and this is the truth.

"But if he does?" She searches my eyes so deeply that I wonder if she really thinks he might. Would she be sad to see me go? Would she try to prevent me?

"You know, Rose, you will always have a place here." She is speaking slowly, the words an effort to release: "This House... I– I had hoped my daughter..."

I touch her hand and she says no more. She nods and goes on her way, and I finish my arrangement.

May loves me, in her way. But as she leaves me, I am thinking about the girl I found on the doorstep of Madame's House; and about Iris's daughter, Anne; and about how Madame has still never asked me to tell her my story.

It is August. Nine months after their victory at Smithton, the Wahnese have cleared the remaining resistance from the region and installed a new governor. They are provisioning for their march, and troops head west—home—each day.

It must be drawing near, the day when the rest of the men will depart, so I am childishly pleased when the prince seems in no hurry to leave.

One evening as we eat, my curiosity overcomes my caution, and I ask him: "Do you miss your home?"

He made a noise that was a scoffing.

"Don't you want to go back there?"

"It matters little to me where I am."

I swallow, unsure. I had not considered the possibility that he might want to remain east. "Then you will stay around Smithton?"

He looks at me a long while, quiet. I cannot read his face—I have never been able to. Finally he says, "No. It matters little to me, but it matters much to others where I am. I will go back."

Ever since the afternoon I understood what I wanted, I've feared I won't have enough time to make it happen. Because I know that deciding alone cannot turn a daydream into a reality. The women here can whisper speculations about the prince's intentions and my future, but I know (as they should): you cannot force the will of another to conform to your own desire.

Still, that night I coax the prince to me a second time, trying to knot him to me.

Madame asks me to take a chain of hers to the goldsmith to be repaired.

Usually I enjoy getting outside the House, but this afternoon is sweltering and humid. Nevertheless, I dress and walk there and drop off the chain as she requested, then return to the House, exhausted.

I pause at the foot of the stairs in the hall to

catch my breath before going up to my room to rest. I can feel the heat coming off my face, like a fever.

Madame passes by, and hastily I compose myself.

"What's the matter with you? Are you unwell?" she asks. Her thumb is not on my chin this time, but I feel the memory of it as much as if it were there.

The smell of her perfume and the incense that lingers in the hall are making me nauseous, but I answer, brightly as I can: "I'm fine, May, thank you."

In fact I am fairly sure I know what ails me, besides the heat. But she nods a dismissal, and I continue to my room, where I quickly find the fresh air of the open window and try to find my appetite.

Today the prince has stopped by in the afternoon. We are standing at the window sipping the wine he brought.

No other guests are yet around, and the girls in the rest of the House are still at their ease. From time to time through our walls can be heard squeals and laughter, and a tone of congratulations in the girls' voices. It must be Columbine, sharing her news.

"One of our girls is to leave with one of your officers," I explain to the prince. "Columbine." She's been on a cloud since matters were arranged. She and he had started about the same time as the prince and I had, three months ago.

But the prince already knows this. "Yes, Captain Nerian." He pauses, then adds: "He has a nice estate in the country. She'll be comfortable."

His words reassure me a little, though I know Columbine's happiness is still far from certain. Then I wonder about my happiness.

I feel a fluttering inside me, like a moth against

the wrong side of a pane in some fine house, and I think that this is when the question should rise, if it is meant to.

But the prince does not ask if I will come with him when he goes.

I finish my wine and take a deep, calm breath, for this is all right: I would not make a good mistress. And I realize (though this is well beside the point) I am not sure I love him.

Accepting all this, I set down my glass, kiss his cheek, and step away from the window. I have grown fond of the prince, yes. I am grateful to him for his part in reviving me. I will take what time we have left.

I slip out of my robe, lie back on the bed, and wait for him to join me.

The last time that he comes to Madame's, I do not know it is the last time until after he has pulled on his boots to go.

He has stayed late into the morning—it is nearly noon. From the bed I watched him dress. I am still tangled in the sheets, elbow-propped and blinking against the bright light that the flimsy curtain does not keep out.

He steps to the window, gazing out where I look. Where some nights he has stood with me, quiet.

"What is out there, down that road?" he asks. "Is that where your sadness started?"

He looks at me, and I wonder what he sees. And then I wonder how many men have seen me standing in that place, looking out of this window.

He is the only one who ever asked me my story.

Part of me wants to tell him why I walked that road and what I fled from. But then I think about how in all these nights we have lain here together he has never told me *his* stories: how his love died, or what she was to him; and why a prince, a king's son, was sent to this inglorious place to fight beside common men; and how he came to trust no one, and why he drinks only his own wine.

Perhaps he would have told me these things, had I but asked. Or maybe some part of me knew from the beginning to let him keep his stories and secrets so I would feel no obligation to trade mine, one for one.

Still, for a candle-flicker's time I consider telling him. He seems an honest man. Do I not owe him the truth?

No. This was no part of his bargain with me. And I neither want nor need anything more from him—not his permission, and not his forgiveness.

"You're going?" I ask. "Today?"

"Yes." He looks down, awkward as the first time he visited me. "I doubt I will pass this way again."

He steps back from the window, and the room brightens. I blink at the light hitting my eye.

I stand, covering myself carefully with the sheet. It is time to be formal again. I bow a good-bye: "Safe journey, your highness."

"Be well, my lady." He leans to me, kisses my cheek, and goes.

The door shuts, and I sit back against the pillows.

That is that, then.

He was gentlemanly. Direct. Noble in his sadness. Though I cannot claim these traits make him a good man.

I hardly knew him. But then, sometimes that makes it easier to love.

Hope revived is a fragile, fledgling thing, but mine is

not shattered by the prince's departure.

Madame inspects me for signs of disappointment but sees none. Indeed, a calm has settled over me. She thinks it is acceptance.

She tells me that soon we will sit down and go over the books. It's time someone else took over the recordkeeping, she says.

"Of course," I tell her, but I know I will act soon. I am just waiting for my moment.

Days after the last Wahnese leave, a client dies at the House—Master Arthur the merchant, a regular, whose heart could not keep up with his lust.

He was with Grace at the time. Hysterical, she called me to her room where he lay, his limbs ridiculous and defeated, his eyes staring but unseeing.

I slide his eyelids closed, tilt his chin until his mouth shuts, and pull the sheet over his nakedness.

"This has happened before," I assure Grace. "You're not to blame."

I send for the steward and Madame. But even as I am sitting Grace down and pouring the wine to steady her, my mind is racing.

She is avoiding looking at the dead man, so it is easy to reach under the sheet, slide the signet from poor Arthur's cold finger, and hide it in the hem of my robe before Madame arrives.

Madame thanks me for my help in the crisis, my quick thinking. She is grateful for how I have started taking care of everything, just as she would have done.

In the morning, when she is seeing to the man's funeral, I go outside for some air. I wait until I am sure no one is watching me, then remove my stash of coins from under the brick in the courtyard wall.

That afternoon, when Madame and Millie think I am in my room resting, I sew the coins into the lining of my bodice, padding each from the others so they will make no sound.

The House is closed that night, the genteel sign of respect that Madame's clients expect after such an occurrence. We Ladies will have an unexpectedly quiet night, alone in our rooms.

I slip out early in the morning, as soon as the city gates will be opened. I had told Millie I wanted to sleep in, so the House won't learn I am missing for a few hours.

I head southeast and Smithton shrinks behind me. At the Qwel market, I purchase what I need and ask the way to Oakton. A farmer and his wife are returning to their village along the way. With a penny I buy a ride that far with them, then continue walking on my own.

The sun starts to set. Every now and then a pretty white pebble, smooth as an egg, catches my eye in that deepening dark. I pick up each one, as deliberately as if it is a piece of something broken that I can mend.

I spend the night at an inn in the last village before Oakton. In the morning, I put on Arthur's ring and change into the dress I bought in Qwel. As I walk the final miles, the black fabric billows over the hill of my belly, which I no longer need to hide.

Master Arthur was (as I have said) a talker, and as I come to Oakton, I recognize his place from his descriptions: the orchard the house looks out over, and the well next to the shed, and the small but comfortable shop.

I let myself in the house. Everything is so tidy,

so clean, waiting for him to return. I feel badly he will never see any of it again.

Within an hour of my arrival, the neighbors have come to see who I am and where he is. I invent a lawful relationship for us and a nobler death for him. I allude to the marks of his body modestly but precisely enough to convince his family and childhood friends that I am indeed his widow, secretly wed five months back on his last business trip through Smithton. "A whirlwind romance." I blush, then cry. I have nothing near Luna's talent, but I am enough of an actress for this. Master Arthur's ring, my belly, and my tears prove my story.

Arthur's community accepts my lie, too polite to mention that such a talkative man never wrote or spoke of me. I think they feel good to take me in, a poor familyless widow, in my condition. I am a place for both grief and hope to rest. Perhaps, too, I am a way they can atone for other guilts.

I have never been so loved, so accepted. I love them back, as openly.

Arthur's sister teaches me what she knows, and I learn the merchant trade as quickly as I forget my previous one.

I put myself together again, like a bird gathers twigs for a nest, and wait for my baby to come.

Rebecca Lartigue teaches literature at Springfield College. Last year the Springfield Cultural Council (a local division of the Massachusetts Cultural Council) awarded her an Artist Fellowship in support of her fiction. Her work has appeared in *The Speculative Edge* and is forthcoming in *Massachusetts Review*. She can be reached via the contact page at www.rebeccalartigue.com.